SCIENCE FICTION

Frances Ridley

Rising Stars UK Ltd.
22 Grafton Street, London W1S 4EX
www.risingstars-uk.com

Helping Everyone Achieve

NASEN House, 4/5 Amber Business Village, Amber Close, Amington,
Tamworth, Staffordshire B77 4RP

Every effort has been made to trace copyright holders and obtain their permission for the use of copyright materials. The publisher will gladly receive information enabling them to rectify any error or omission in subsequent editions.

All facts are correct at time of going to press.

The right of Frances Ridley to be identified as the author of this work has been asserted by her in accordance with the Copyright, Design and Patents Act 1988.

Published 2008

Text, design and layout © Rising Stars UK Ltd.
Series Consultant: Lorraine Petersen
Cover design: Neil Straker Creative
Cover photograph: Alamy
Design: Geoff Rayner, Bag of Badgers
Editorial: Frances Ridley
Photographs:
AKG Images: 8, 16, 30, 45
Alamy: 12, 16, 32
BBC Photo Library: 14, 34, 35
Kobal Collection: 4, 10, 11, 13, 16, 17, 18, 19, 20, 22-23, 24-25, 26-27, 28-29, 32, 33, 36, 38, 40-41, 41, 42, 44, 46, 47

British Library Cataloguing in Publication Data.
A CIP record for this book is available from the British Library.

ISBN: 978-1-84680-446-5

Printed by: Craftprint International Ltd, Singapore

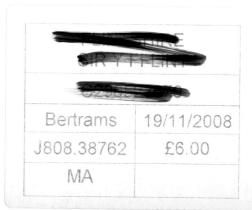

CONTENTS

SCIENCE FICTION: THE BIG PICTURE

Some science fiction stories are set in space. Other science fiction stories are set in the future. Science fiction stories can be about robots, aliens, or people with special powers.

FOCUS

FIND OUT THE ANSWERS TO THESE QUESTIONS.

1   WHAT DO THE LETTERS FTL STAND FOR?

2   WHAT IS THE DOCTOR'S TIME MACHINE CALLED?

3   HOW DO THE ALIENS TRAVEL ABOUT IN WAR OF THE WORLDS?

ZOOMING IN...

Virtual World
The matrix is out there.

War in Space
May the Force
be with you.

Aliens
They're not all bad!

Space Travel
On board the
Starship Enterprise.

Time Travel
Going back to the future.

Robots and AI
Don't let them take over!

Invasion!
A virus saves the day.

SPACE TRAVEL

MANY SCIENCE FICTION STORIES
ARE ABOUT SPACE TRAVEL.
STAR TREK IS ABOUT A STARSHIP
CALLED ENTERPRISE.
THE SHIP AND ITS CREW TRAVEL
ACROSS THE UNIVERSE.
ITS MISSION IS TO EXPLORE SPACE AND
MAKE CONTACT WITH OTHER PLANETS.

Jonathan Archer
Captain of the
Enterprise NX-01

A great day – **Enterprise** NX-01 set off on its first deep space mission.

Enterprise is our fastest starship. It has a warp-five engine. It can travel to planets that we've never been to before.

The ship has two shuttle pods. These can't travel at warp speed. The crew will use them to visit nearby planets or other starships. There is also a **transporter system**. This can beam cargo to and from the ship. It can also beam people – but the crew don't want to try it out!

ENTERPRISE NX-01

SAUCER

BRIDGE

NX-01

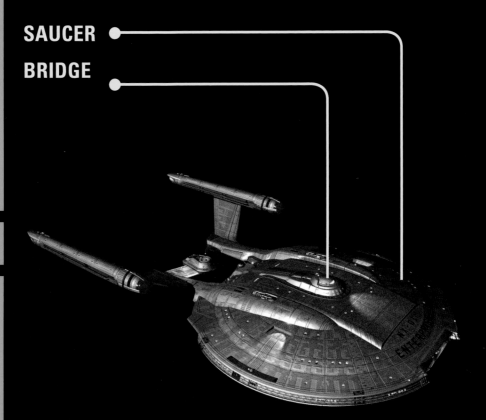

There are 83 crew members. Most of them work in the large saucer. I spend most of my time on the bridge – the command centre of the ship!

FTL SPEEDS

Space travel isn't easy in real life.

It takes months or years to travel to other planets.

AN **UNMANNED SPACE CRAFT** ON MARS.

In science fiction stories, starships travel at FTL speeds.

FTL stands for 'faster than light'.

Starships cross galaxies in minutes rather than years.

FTL FOCUS

STARSHIPS IN STAR TREK USE WARP DRIVE TO GO AT FTL SPEED.

STARSHIPS IN STAR WARS USE HYPERDRIVE TO GO AT FTL SPEED.

TIME TRAVEL

THERE ARE LOTS OF WAYS TO TRAVEL
IN TIME IN SCIENCE FICTION.
IN MANY STORIES, PEOPLE TRAVEL IN
A TIME MACHINE. THESE MACHINES CAN
TRAVEL TO THE PAST OR THE FUTURE.

TIME MACHINE TIMELINE

1963

Doctor Who (TV Series)

Doctor Who's TARDIS:

- takes him to any point in time or space
- looks like a police box
- is much bigger on the inside than it is on the outside.

1895

The Time Machine (Novel)

The very first time machine.

2007

Meet the Robinsons (Film)

This time machine can fly!

Back to the Future (Film)

This time machine:

- needs 1.21 **gigawatts** of power to work
- is set to travel to a target date
- has to reach 88 mph to travel in time.

1989

Bill and Ted's Excellent Adventure (Film)

This time machine looks like a phone box, too – but it's not bigger on the inside than it is on the outside!

TIME TRAVELLERS

Time travel can be tricky. Time travellers get into all sorts of trouble. Sometimes they get stuck in the past. Sometimes they change the past and that changes the future!

BACK TO THE FUTURE

The main character in this film is Marty.

He goes back in time to 1955.

Marty finds out that he has to help his parents get together.

If he fails, he won't be born!

ROBOTS AND AI

MANY SCIENCE FICTION STORIES HAVE ROBOTS. SOMETIMES, THE ROBOTS ARE **PROGRAMMED** BY HUMANS. THEY CAN ONLY DO WHAT HUMANS TELL THEM TO DO.

SOMETIMES, THE ROBOTS HAVE AI – **ARTIFICIAL** INTELLIGENCE. THEY CAN THINK FOR THEMSELVES AND DO WHATEVER THEY WANT TO.

WHAT ROBOT?

Issue 200. The Big Robot Quiz...

Does your robot have AI?

Which of these best describes your robot?

> My robot
>
> a.　never laughs at jokes.
>
> b.　laughs at jokes.
>
> c.　makes its own jokes.

> My robot
>
> a.　doesn't understand when I am angry.
>
> b.　gets upset when I am angry.
>
> c.　gets angry back!

> My robot
>
> a.　doesn't have dreams.
>
> b.　wants to hear about my dreams.
>
> c.　has dreams and tells me about them.

If your scores were mainly a:

You have a perfectly normal robot.

If your scores were mainly b:

You robot is showing some signs of AI.
Keep an eye on it but don't worry.

If your scores were mainly c:

Your robot has AI. It is important to give it
a good **role model**. Take care of your robot
and show it how to behave well.

JUST LIKE US!

Intelligent robots in science fiction stories can be good or bad – just like humans.

I, ROBOT

In this film, most people have a robot.

The robots are programmed to obey humans and not to harm them. The story begins when a man is found dead.

Detective Spooner thinks that a robot called Sonny murdered the man. Sonny has dreams and feels fear and anger. He doesn't always obey humans.

Sonny tells Spooner that he didn't murder the man – but is he telling the truth?

CLOSE UP: ALIEN INVASION

THE TRIPODS FIRE DEATH RAYS

THE ALIENS MOVE AROUND IN HUGE TRIPODS

In *War of the Worlds*, the Earth is invaded by aliens from Mars. The aliens nearly win.
Then they catch a human **virus** – the common cold. The aliens die because they can't fight the virus.

In *Independence Day*, huge alien spaceships come to invade Earth. The aliens aren't beaten by a human virus in this story. Instead, the humans use a computer virus to help them win the war.

NEW YORK

HUGE ALIEN SPACESHIPS HOVER OVER THE WORLD'S CITIES

ALIENS

MANY SCIENCE FICTION STORIES ARE ABOUT ALIENS.

SOME ALIENS ARE FRIENDLY AND OTHERS
ARE HOSTILE.

SOME ALIENS LOOK LIKE US AND OTHERS DON'T
LOOK LIKE ANY OTHER EARTH CREATURE!

SOME ALIENS ACT LIKE US AND OTHERS
HAVE SPECIAL POWERS.

ALIEN ID CARDS

ET

Home planet:
Not known.

Description:
Small and friendly with a glowing finger.

Other information:
Used mind-power to make a bicycle fly in *ET*.

DALEKS

Home planet:
Skaro.

Description:
Mutant killers in metal cases.

Other information:
Wiped out the Time Lord race in *Doctor Who*.

EWOKS

Home planet:
Planet Endor's moon.

Description:
Strong and furry with big eyes.

Other information:
Used Stone-Age weapons to beat the Stormtroopers in *Return of the Jedi.*

MR SPOCK

Home planet:
Vulcan.

Description:
Loyal and logical with pointed ears.

Other information:
Uses a Vulcan neck pinch to knock people out in *Star Trek.*

TRANSFORMERS

Home planet:
Cybertron.

Description:
Alien robots that can change into machines.

Other information:
Come in two types – Autobots are good and Decepticons are bad.

ALIENS AND HUMANS

It's not always easy to tell humans and aliens apart.
In *Doctor Who*, the Doctor looks and acts like
a human – but he's an alien.

THE DOCTOR IS A TIME LORD.

HE HAS TWO HEARTS.

DR WHO

In one episode, the Doctor and Rose travel to the year five billion. They go to a party. The guests are different aliens. They are going to watch the end of the Earth!

One guest says that she is the last human. She has changed her body so much that she looks like an alien.

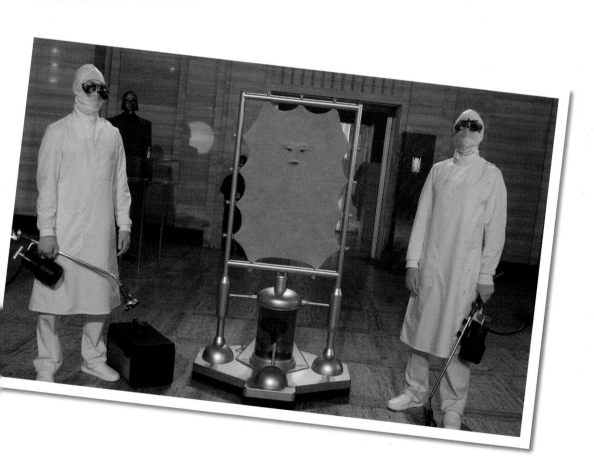

WAR IN SPACE

IN SOME SCIENCE FICTION STORIES, SPACE TRAVEL IS EASY. DIFFERENT PLANETS IN A GALAXY ARE LIKE DIFFERENT COUNTRIES ON EARTH. THEY TRADE WITH EACH OTHER AND THEY GO TO WAR WITH EACH OTHER.

Star Wars – A New Hope (1977)

Review

By **Sci-Fi Fan** - see my other reviews

A New Hope is about a far away galaxy. The galaxy is ruled by an evil Empire but a group of rebels are fighting back.

Darth Vadar is building the Death Star.
This huge space station is the size of a planet.
Vadar wants to use it to crush the rebellion.

Luke Skywalker is a farm boy. He gets a
message from a rebel called Princess Leia.
He leaves his planet on a mission to rescue
the Princess – and join the rebels!

A New Hope came out in 1977 as *Star Wars*.
Its SFX were cutting-edge at the time. It looks
dated now – but it's still a great story!
To my mind, none of the other *Star Wars* films
come close.

 Average Review

Was this review helpful to you?

STAR WARS

The war in the *Star Wars* films is between the Jedi and the Sith. The Jedi fight for good and the Sith fight for evil. Both sides use a power called the Force.

The Force is very strong in Anakin Skywalker.

The Jedi train him to fight for good. But Anakin is angry and confused.

He joins the Sith and begins to fight for evil.

Anakin fights his Jedi teacher and almost dies.

The Sith save him and Anakin becomes Darth Vadar.

VIRTUAL WORLDS

MANY MODERN SCIENCE FICTION STORIES ARE ABOUT VIRTUAL WORLDS. THESE ARE WORLDS CREATED BY COMPUTERS.

IN SOME STORIES, PEOPLE CHOOSE TO ENTER THE VIRTUAL WORLD.

IN OTHER STORIES, PEOPLE DON'T KNOW THAT THEY ARE IN A VIRTUAL WORLD!

What's Your Problem?

Dear Crystal,

I'm so worried. My life doesn't feel right – it doesn't feel real. Am I mad?

Yours,

Thomas Anderson

Dear Mr Anderson,

You're not mad. Sadly, machines have taken over our world. They have plugged us into a huge computer. We think we're living in a real world – but it's a computer image. The machines want to keep us happy because they need our energy. They use human energy to make electricity.

This must be a shock for you. Please find Morpheus if you are unhappy. He is the leader of a band of rebels in the 'real' world. He's very keen to meet you. He thinks you can help the rebels fight the machines.

Good luck,

Crystal Ball

Morpheus

THE MATRIX

In this film, humans are trapped in a computer world called the Matrix. Thomas Anderson escapes and joins a band of rebels. In the 'real world' he is called Neo. He helps the rebels win The Machine War.

In the 'real world', the rebels are normal people. Life is hard. The food is bad and they wear tatty clothes.

In the Matrix, the rebels wear smart clothes. They have special powers. They are strong and fast, and they are excellent fighters.

GLOSSARY

Artificial   Man-made.

Gigawatts   'Giga' means one thousand million and a watt is a unit of power. So Gigawatts means a lot of power!

Mutant   Something that has changed from the way it used to be

Programmed   Putting information into a machine or a robot.

Role model   A person that you can copy to learn good behaviour.

Transporter system A way of moving people and things from one place to another.

Unmanned space craft A space craft that doesn't have any human passengers.

Virus   A human virus spreads disease or infection; a computer virus destroys information.

INDEX